THE GOLDEN SERPENT

by

WALTER DEAN MYERS

illustrated by

ALICE AND MARTIN
PROVENSEN

The Viking Press   *New York*

For Amarjit Mangat

A. & M. P.

First Edition
Text Copyright © Walter Dean Myers, 1980
Illustrations Copyright © Alice and Martin Provensen, 1980
All rights reserved
First published in 1980 by The Viking Press
625 Madison Avenue, New York, New York 10022
Published simultaneously in Canada by Penguin Books Canada Limited
Printed in U.S.A.
1 2 3 4 5 84 83 82 81 80

Library of Congress Cataloging in Publication Data
Myers, Walter Dean. The golden serpent.
Summary: The wise man Pundabi tries to help the
king see the poverty and suffering in his
kingdom by solving the mystery of the Golden Serpent.
[1. Fables] I. Provensen, Alice. II. Provensen, Martin. III. Title.
PZ8.2.M9Go [E] 80-12731 ISBN 0-670-34445-1

The art for this book was prepared in acrylic paints and
pen and ink. The text typeface is Palatino; the display
typeface is Centaur.

THE GOLDEN SERPENT

THERE was once a very wise man. He lived on a high
mountain and was called Pundabi. With him lived a
young boy. The boy's name was Ali.

Each morning Ali would come down the mountain.
He would sit in the shade of a fig tree. Many people
would come to him. They brought him loaves of bread.
In the bread were pieces of fine linen. There would be
questions on the linen for the wise Pundabi to answer.
They would be questions of life and death, or
about the search for happiness.

Each evening Ali would climb the mountain and give
the loaves of bread to Pundabi. Pundabi would answer
all the questions. Then they would eat the bread.

Ali would take the answers down the mountain. He would give them to the waiting people. Pundabi and Ali lived well this way, and the people loved them dearly.

One day a tall shadow fell across Ali. It was the shadow of the king himself.

"Are you Ali?" the king asked.

"I am he," Ali answered.

"And you live with the wise man Pundabi?"

"That is so," Ali replied.

"And it is true that he is very wise?"

"Yes, it is true," said Ali.

"Then you must bring him to me," the king said.

So Ali went up the mountain. He told Pundabi of the
king's request. Pundabi and Ali came down the mountain. They set out for the palace. They went past the
river and through the marketplace. They went through the
village. Finally they reached another high mountain.

On top of this mountain was the palace.

"I want you to solve a mystery for me." The king spoke from his high throne. "But first we must have lunch." He clapped his hands twice.

Five men brought in five trays of food. There was a
tray for Pundabi. There was a tray for Ali. And three
trays for the king.

"I am very rich," the king said. "I have much gold and many rubies. And you, Pundabi, are very wise. I can pay you very well."

"What is the mystery?" asked Pundabi.

"I do not know," said the king. "That is for you to discover!"

"But how can Pundabi solve a mystery "—Ali wrung his hands—"if there is none to solve?"

"If you are truly wise, Pundabi, it will be done. If you do not solve it, then you are a fraud. I will put you in jail where you belong."

Ali was very afraid. He began to shake.

But Pundabi said, "Let us take a walk. Perhaps our
eyes will speak to us."
So they began to walk. They walked by the river.

They walked through the village. They stopped by the home of an old woman. They walked around the market-place. Pundabi's eyes spoke to him.

Then Pundabi began to walk up the mountain toward the palace.

"We will surely go to jail," Ali said. "We cannot solve the mystery. We do not know what it is."

"But we do know what the mystery is." Pundabi spoke, a smile upon his face. "And perhaps we can solve it. Let us go and see the king."

"Have you solved the mystery yet?" the king asked.

"No," said Pundabi. "But we know what the mystery is! It is the mystery of the Golden Serpent."

"The Golden Serpent?" said the king.

"Yes," Pundabi said. "Where is your Golden Serpent?"

"I didn't know I had one," the king said.

"The thief must be very clever," Pundabi said.

"You must find it for me," said the king.

"Let us see," Pundabi said. "Someone must have taken it to sell. Let us go to the market."

So the king called his guards. And off they went to the market.

In the market they came upon a young boy. The boy was turning wood.

"Perhaps he has stolen the Golden Serpent." The king seized the boy by the arm.

"I have no Golden Serpent," the boy said. "I could not run away with it. My leg is bent from turning."

But the guards searched him well. They searched his blouse and the hay upon which he slept. They even looked at his bent leg.

"It is true," the guards said. "He has nothing. He can hardly walk."

Next they went to the village. They stopped at the house of a widow.

"We are searching for the Golden Serpent," said Pundabi, "which was stolen from the king."

"I do not have it," said the widow. "I have only this small cup of grain."

But the king did not trust her. So the guards searched her hut. They looked in the corners. They looked in the cupboard.

"It is true," said the guards. "She has nothing but this cup of grain."

"Let us go from this dismal place," the king said.

Outside they heard a strange cry. Three men walked together. They sang a sad song. The first had a stick. He swung it before him as he walked. The second walked behind the first. The third walked behind the second. Each had a hand on the other's shoulder.

"Perhaps," said Pundabi, "these are your thieves."

"These?" said the king. "Why, they cannot see!"

"How clever of them," said Pundabi.

So they stopped the three blind men and asked of the king's Golden Serpent.

"No," said the first. "I have only this stick for comfort."

"No," said the second. "I have only the few coins I am given."

"No," said the third. "I have but these two friends."

But the king did not trust them. So the guards searched the three blind men.

"They have nothing," said the guards, "except a worm-eaten stick and a few coins. Nothing more."

"Let us return to the palace," the king said.

"But we have not found the Golden Serpent," Pundabi said.

"I no longer want it," the king said bitterly. "I will pay you and you can leave."

At the palace, the king had his counters pay Pundabi in gold coins.

"And what about your people?" Pundabi asked.

"My people?" asked the king.

"Yes. The crippled boy, the poor widow, and the blind beggars," said Ali.

"What about them, indeed!" said the king. "They did not find my Golden Serpent."

"Ah," said Pundabi, "I see. But I have solved your mystery. I know where the Golden Serpent is."

"You do?" said the king. "How splendid!"

"You must close your eyes and count slowly until you reach a hundred. But make sure you are alone so that no one can steal the Golden Serpent again. Then open your eyes. The Golden Serpent will be in your room."

The king closed his eyes and began to count slowly as Pundabi picked up his bag of gold and left the palace.

He went down the steep hill.
He gave some of the gold to the crippled boy.

He gave some to the widow.   He gave some to the blind beggars.

"Pundabi," said Ali. "You are both wise and generous. But there is still one problem."

"And what is that?" asked Pundabi.

"When the king opens his eyes," said Ali, "he will still not find the Golden Serpent."

"No," said Pundabi. "Some people never do. But that is another mystery."